I'M Happy
and Other Fun Feelings

Clare Hibbert
Illustrated by Simona Dimitri

amicus

This title has been published with the co-operation of Cherrytree Books
Amicus Illustrated is published by Amicus
P.O. Box 1329, Mankato, Minnesota 56002

Printed in Mankato, Minnesota, USA by CG Book Printers, a division of
Corporate Graphics

Library of Congress Cataloging-in-Publication Data

Hibbert, Clare, 1970-
I'm happy and other fun feelings / Clare Hibbert ; illustrated by Simona Dimitri.
    p. cm. -- (Feelings)
Includes index.
ISBN 978-1-60753-173-9 (library binding)
1. Happiness in children--Juvenile literature. 2. Emotions in children--Juvenile
literature. I. Dimitri, Simona. II. Title.
BF723.H37H55 2011
152.4--dc22
                                    2011002245

13-digit ISBN: 978-1-60753-173-9 First Edition 1110987654321
First published in 2010 by Evans Brothers Ltd.
2A Portman Mansions, Chiltern Street, London W1U 6NR, United Kingdom

CONTENTS

wheeeee

Whoooosh!

glad proud interested kind calm

5

Brave

In my game I fought a dragon. I felt very **brave**.

Swish

happy

brave

safe

excited

Rooooooar!

Safe

choo choo!

happy

brave

safe

excited

Excited

Happy Birthday to you!

My friend invited me to her party. I was very **excited**.

10

happy   brave   safe   excited

♪ ♪ Happy Birthday to you! ♪ ♪ ♪ ♪

glad

proud

interested

kind

calm

Glad

squeak

happy

brave

safe

excited

12

Proud

I made Grandad **proud**. He was a good swimmer too.

14

happy

brave

safe

excited

splish splash!

glad   proud   interested   kind   calm

15

Interested

eeek!

WOW!

16

happy

brave

safe

excited

I visited the museum with my class. I felt **interested**.

glad proud interested kind calm

17

What a kind boy.

glad   proud   interested   kind   calm

19

Calm

happy

brave

safe

excited

I was worried, so I thought of something **calm**.

whoosh

glad

proud

interested

kind

calm

Notes for adults

The **Feelings** series has been designed to support and extend the learning of young children. The books tie in with teaching strategies for reading with children. Find out more from the International Reading Association (www.reading.org), and The National Association for the education of Young Children (www.naeyc.org).

The **Feelings...** series helps to develop children's knowledge, understanding, and skills in key social and emotional aspects of learning, in particular empathy, self-awareness, and social skills. It aims to help children understand, articulate, and manage their feelings.

Titles in the series:
I'm Happy and Other Fun Feelings looks at positive emotions
I'm Sad and Other Tricky Feelings looks at uncomfortable emotions
I'm Tired and Other Body Feelings looks at physical feelings
I'm Busy a Feelings Story explores other familiar feelings

The **Feelings...** books offer the following special features:

1) **matching game**
   a border of expressive faces gives readers the chance to hunt out the face that matches the emotion covered on the spread;
2) **fantasy scenes**
   since children often explore emotion through stories, dreams and their imaginations, two emotions (in this book, "brave" and "calm") are presented in a fantasy setting, giving the opportunity to examine intense feelings in the safety of an unreal context.

Making the most of reading time
When reading with younger children, take time to explore the pictures together. Ask children to find, identify, count, or describe different objects. Point out colors and textures. Pause in your reading so that children can ask questions, repeat your words, or even predict the next word. This sort of participation develops early reading skills.

Follow the words with your finger as you read. The main text is in Infant Sassoon, a clear, friendly font designed for children learning to read and write. The thought and speech bubbles and sound effects add fun and give the opportunity to distinguish between levels of communication.

Extend children's learning by using this book as a springboard for discussion and follow-up activities. Here are a few ideas:

Pages 4–5: Happy

Ask children to keep a happiness diary for a week. Divide a sheet of paper into seven areas, and write the names of the days. Each day, the children can record things that made them happy by drawing or sticking on something (for example, an ice cream wrapper or a photo).

Pages 6–7: Brave

Use a selection of art materials to make a gigantic dragon mural — egg boxes make excellent 3D scales. Find a retelling of "George and the Dragon." How many other dragon stories do the children know? Do they believe dragons are real or not? What other pretend monsters can they think of?

Pages 8–9: Safe

Discuss why someone might feel scared in the school or daycare setting. Think together of ways to make it safe and accessible to all. Could a mentoring system work? Encourage the children to make clothespin "emotion dolls" that they can use to express difficult feelings and explore tricky situations — for example, at circle time.

Pages 10–11: Excited

Stick 12 big circles on the wall. Label each with the name of a month. Ask each child to put a named drawing or photo of him- or herself in the correct birthday month (to adapt for home, show birthdays of family and friends). What other events in the year are exciting? Add illustrated markers for festivals such as Chinese New Year, Holi, Easter, Id-ul-Fitr, Divali, Guru Nanak, Kwanzaa, Christmas and Hanukkah.

Pages 12–13: Glad

Make up a simple "welcome home" song — or teach the words to "For s/he's a jolly good fellow." Encourage the children to accompany the singing with a selection of percussion, and discuss how the joyful music expresses the feeling of gladness.

Pages 14–15: Proud

Cut out aluminum foil circles and ask children to draw on simple icons to represent activities that they do well (such as a soccer ball, bicycle, paintbrush, or pair of swimming goggles). Attach the "medals of achievement" to colored ribbons so they can be worn around the children's necks.

Pages 16–17: Interested

Can children think of the word that means the opposite of "interested"? Children can create a pairs game by illustrating cards with opposite emotions or states: for example, happy/sad, quiet/noisy, sleepy/wide awake, interested/bored.

Pages 18–19: Kind

Encourage children to draw a plan of their school or daycare to help newcomers find their way. Mark the entrance, and use pictures cut out from magazines to illustrate key places (for example, restrooms, lunchroom, reading area, and playground).

Pages 20–21: Calm

Ask each child to imagine a calm, happy scene that they can think about whenever they feel worried or frightened — for example, after a bad dream. Then provide paints and collage materials so children can recreate their imaginings for a display.

Index

Credits

The publisher would like to thank the following for permission to reproduce their images:
iStockphoto: cover and 4–5 (Peter Garbet), 4 (Cebas), 6–7 (Dave Block), 6 (Stiggdriver), 8 (mammamaart), 10–11 (ptaxa), 10 (hidesy), 12–13 (Ramsey Blacklock), 12 (tirc83), 14–15 (Lugo Graphics), 14 (klikk), 16–17 (Jello5700), 18–19 (Eric Ferguson), 18 (VisualField), 21 (jacomstephens); **Shutterstock Images:** 7 (Sandra van der Steen), 8–9 (Hannamariah), 16 (zaharch), 20–21 (Centrill Media), 20 (Christopher Ewing).